LITTLE
PENGUiN
RESCUE

tiger tales

5 River Road, Suite 128, Wilton, CT 06897
Published in the United States 2020
Originally published in Great Britain 2019
by the Little Tiger Group
Text copyright © 2019 Rachel Delahaye
Inside illustrations copyright © 2019 Jo Anne Davies at Artful Doodlers
Cover illustration copyright © 2019 Suzie Mason
ISBN-13: 978-1-68010-467-7
ISBN-10: 1-68010-467-5
Printed in the USA
STP/4800/0337/0720
10 9 8 7 6 5 4 3 2 1

For more insight and activities, visit us at www.tigertalesbooks.com

LITTLE
PENGUIN
RESCUE

by Rachel Delahaye

tiger tales

For Elise and Fleur, who love birds of all feathers
—Rachel

CONTENTS

Cold Play

"It's snowing! It's snowing!" Emma was shouting so loudly that Callie had to hold the phone away from her ear. "This is the best day of my life!"

"You said that last time it snowed!" Callie replied, watching the thick flakes falling outside the window.

"Yes, but this snow day is going to be the best. We're going to go sledding down the street and throw snowballs in the yard and drink hot chocolate."

"And get wet bottoms again?" Callie giggled, remembering how last time they had slipped off their plastic-bag sleds and skidded down the street laughing.

"Maybe not that," said Emma. "But all the rest of it, definitely! I'll be over as soon as I've had breakfast."

"Okay, see you soon!"

Callie grinned as she put down the phone and pulled on her coat, gloves, and boots. She couldn't wait to tell her neighbors, Kamal and Halima, that Emma was on her way. They could all have a huge snowball fight!

When she opened the back door, the cold hit her face with an icy blast. She blinked away the snowflakes and stepped out into a world she hardly recognized. It was as if a huge white blanket had been thrown over everything. Thick snow had settled on the tops of the fences. Tree branches bowed under its weight. Smaller bushes were completely covered so that they looked like strange, lumpy white monsters.

Callie hoped all the wild animals had found somewhere safe and warm to stay, because except for the crunch of her footsteps on the fresh snow, there was no sound. It was all so peaceful. Almost too peaceful…. Just a few minutes ago, she had heard Kamal and Halima screaming and laughing outside. Where were they now?

"Hey, Catalina!"

It was Kamal. He always called her by her full name.

"I've told you before—friends call me Callie!" she said, still unable to see him.

"We're not friends," came the reply. "Not when we're having a snowball fight!"

Suddenly—*WHOOSH!*—a snowball zoomed past Callie's head. It was an ambush! Kamal and Halima had been hiding all this time, waiting for her to step outside. Callie shrieked and ducked as another one flew by.

"Hey! Wait a minute!" she called. Two faces peered over the fence. Callie quickly scooped up a snowball and threw it back at them. It broke apart in midair and showered snow over their heads.

Kamal's eyes twinkled with excitement. There was snow on his nose.

"That's it!" he grinned. "I'm really going to get you now! Come on, Halima, make as many snowballs as you can. We're going to win this fight."

"Emma's coming over soon. You'll be in trouble then!" Callie shouted.

"We'll be two against two," said Halima. Pretty white flakes decorated her dark hair. "That will make it even."

"It'll be nowhere near even. Emma fights like an angry yeti!" laughed Callie.

While she had been talking to Halima, Callie hadn't noticed Kamal picking up two more snowballs. They flew at her now, one hitting her ear.

"Oh, sorry, Callie, did I get you?" Kamal grinned naughtily.

"Yes, you did," Callie said, pretending to be grumpy. "And I don't like being wet and cold."

"I thought you wanted to be a vet when you grow up."

"What does that have to do with being hit by a snowball?" asked Callie.

"Well, vets have to go out in all kinds of weather. If you can't take a little snow, I'm not sure you'll be able to handle being a vet."

Callie wanted to be a vet more than anything, and Kamal knew that. He was smiling, waiting for her reaction.

"I can take snow," she said boldly.

"Take this then!" said Halima, throwing a snowball that hit her on the forehead.

Callie calmly wiped the drips from her eyes and held up her hand. "Wait right there," she said.

"What for?" asked Halima.

"I need my vet equipment to figure out a couple of wild animals—you!" Callie laughed and ran to the shed on the other side of the yard. She planned to get a shovel and a bucket so she could collect a bunch of snow and tip it over the fence and onto their heads.

Inside she found what she needed. She also found a fishing net, which would be perfect for catching snowballs and flinging them back—that would surprise them! Laughing to herself, she opened the door, ready to do battle.

A huge gust of wind forced Callie

to close her
eyes. When
she opened
them, she saw
snow-topped
black mountains
in the distance,
glistening beneath the sun, and a steel-
blue sea littered with what looked like
scrunched-up tissues. Callie's face
tingled, and it was so icy cold that it
took her breath away. She didn't know
where she was—only that she was a
long way from home. Freezing and
a little frightened, Callie went back
inside the shed and closed the door.

The Shed

When Callie had gotten over her shock, she looked around and saw that the shed was no longer filled with plastic plant pots and Dad's rusty tools. It wasn't made of wood anymore, and it definitely wasn't small.

She saw that she was in a hallway with a plastic floor. She walked down it, pushed open a heavy door, and found herself in a large, brightly lit room. There were rugs on the floor and several large couches. She saw some binoculars in the corner and put a pair around her neck. Doors led to other rooms, and there were small round windows looking out at the ocean.

Where on earth was she? Callie put down her bucket and fishing net and started to examine a long desk that held several computers. The machines were on and blinked with information. The first one had a document open on the screen. It read:

The New Captain Scott Research Station.

Survey to measure the effects of rising temperatures on the pack ice of Ross Island, Antarctica.

Antarctica! She really *was* far from home. She was at the South Pole!

And those things that looked like scrunched-up tissues—they were icebergs! *This building must be where the scientists live and work*, Callie thought as she looked around. Although there was nobody here now. Maybe the scientists were out on the ice, taking their measurements.

The Shed

Callie's fear melted away as her attention was drawn to a map on the wall, showing Ross Island. Most of the island was white, and it had very few landmarks—just the names of mountains and peaks, and dots to show the location of various buildings. There weren't many: there was a black dot on the west of the island marked "Shackleton's Hut" and—a-ha!—a red dot below, which meant "You are here." It showed she was inside the New Captain Scott Research Station. Right next door was another dot: "Captain Scott's Hut."

Callie gasped as she absorbed the information. Shackleton was a famous explorer; Captain Scott was even more famous. He made it to the South Pole two years before Shackleton. They had trekked all this way just to see if it was possible. But why had *she* come all this way?

Well, she wouldn't find out by sitting around. She knew that the special thing about the South Pole was its landscape, which had hardly been touched by humans. She needed to get out there and see it for herself! Callie shivered as she remembered the icy blast that had frozen her skin. She was going to need protection.

She looked around and found a wardrobe full of snowsuits, glasses, gloves, and hats. They were too big for her, but she took the smallest-looking suit and slipped it on over her clothes. Then she took a pair of gloves, snow goggles, and a beanie hat. She felt like an astronaut crossed with a giant marshmallow, but it would do for now.

Callie opened the door to the outside and the wind whipped around her ears, whistling loudly. She pulled down her hat, snuggled her face inside the top of her snowsuit, and looked around. She was high off the ground! She hadn't realized the building was raised on stilts. A balcony ran all the way around it, with steps to the ground. When her eyes got used to the bright sunlight, she could see it all clearly.

The South Pole!

There were large pieces of ice floating in the water, and the shore was a mixture of iceblocks, rocks, and brown soil. For a moment, Callie wondered why the ground wasn't covered in snow. Then she realized—it was summer! Of course! She was on the other side of the world. Although summer here was still much colder than any winter at home.

A movement down below grabbed her attention. The earth was shifting. At first she thought it was a trick of the light, but no—the entire shoreline was definitely moving!

Callie went out onto the balcony. She held tightly to the handrail and leaned forward, hoping to find out what was happening. Ideas flashed through her

mind. Maybe it was a landslide, or
lava oozing from a slow-erupting
volcano, or maybe the station was
built on drifting ice.... She thought
about going back inside and using the
radios and computers to call for help.
But suddenly the wind dropped, the
whistling in her ears stopped, and the
air filled with noise. And it wasn't the
creak or crack of land breaking apart.
It sounded more like ducks and geese.

Callie looked again at the moving
mass. After a short time, she started
to see the telltale black-and-white
bodies of ... penguins! So many
penguins! The moving land was a mass
of penguins—hundreds, maybe even
thousands of them.

She lifted the binoculars to her face,

twisting the dials to bring them into
focus. A-ha, there they were! Sweet
black-and-white penguins, waddling
around.

But Callie didn't want to just look
at the birds through binoculars. She
wanted to get up close to them.
Her heart leaped at the thought of
being right there, walking among the
penguins of the South Pole.

She ran inside to return the binoculars. As she was coming back out, she noticed a poster on the wall—*Animals of the Antarctic*. Even though it was summer on this side of the world, she'd seen the outside temperature was 5 degrees. 5! There weren't many animals adapted to that kind of temperature. The poster had pictures of foxes, fishing birds, seals, orcas, and—there!—penguins.

There were only four types of penguin that lived this far south: Emperor, Gentoo, Chinstrap, and Adélie. Callie could see right away that these weren't Emperors—she hadn't noticed any blushes of yellow or orange on their chests or necks. This colony had to be one of the other three types. She memorized the pictures so she could identify them when she was up close.

Feeling a little clumsy in her oversized suit, Callie carefully made her way down the steps. She was going to meet some penguins—her mom's favorite animal! She felt so warm with happiness that she hardly felt the sting of the freezing air.

Laughing with Penguins

As Callie walked toward the penguins, their shapes and features became clear. They didn't have the strange markings of Chinstraps, or the wispy white eyebrows of Gentoos. These were Adélie penguins—small, compact, and jet-black, except for their ice-white tummies. She giggled at their funny white-rimmed, beady eyes. They were just like the googly eyes she used for her craft projects!

Callie walked closer, not knowing how they'd react to a human dressed as a giant marshmallow. She expected them to part to either side of her, frantic with fear, or flap at her, fiercely protecting their families. But the Adélies were too busy to notice her arrival….

Callie couldn't see what they were doing at first. It looked as if they were rounding each other up, but soon she saw they were just playing and bickering.

Suddenly, right in front of her, a little Adélie approached a neat heap of stones that another penguin seemed to be guarding. When the guard penguin turned its back, the little penguin quickly snatched up a stone in its beak and waddled away as casually as it could, as if it hadn't done anything wrong.

The guard penguin spotted the pebble-robber and began chasing it at full speed, with its flippers held out and beak open. Callie imagined it was squawking, "Thief, thief!" While it was chasing the naughty Adélie, other penguins began to take more stones from the unguarded pile. Callie couldn't help laughing.

She also couldn't understand why the penguins were so protective of their stones. It's not as if they were diamonds and pearls! Besides, they were everywhere. Looking more closely, however, Callie noticed that the pebbles were stacked in little piles or laid out in small circles. They were nests! And if they were nests … there must be chicks! But Callie had seen pictures of fluffy gray and white penguin chicks before, and there weren't any here.

Just then, a penguin waddled so close to Callie that it stood on her foot.

"I'm sorry!" she said. "Did I get in your way?"

The penguin ignored her, but Callie saw a clump of tufty gray feathers on its otherwise sleek black head.

"A-ha! So you *are* chicks," Callie said. "But your baby feathers have already molted."

Many of the chicks had lost most of their baby feathers and only had a couple left, sticking out at odd angles on their heads. None of them seemed to have as many as this funny, clumsy penguin. Some had finished molting altogether, and as the chicks waddled and chased and flapped, the downy feathers drifted around Callie like a feather storm.

The chick that had stepped on her foot—the one with baby feathers still stuck to its head—waddled back toward her and stepped on her foot again.

"Hey! Watch where you're going," teased Callie.

The little Adélie lifted its neck to look up at her. It flapped its flippers, made a short sharp honking noise, and scuttled away again.

Callie laughed so loudly that the Adélie stopped and turned around. It honked again. Was it copying her? Callie couldn't stop laughing!

Then she heard another longer, deeper honk behind her, and Callie turned to see an adult penguin running after the little one. It was having trouble because of a foot that seemed to be hurt. Its flipper was damaged, too—ripped halfway down the middle. Callie wondered what had happened. Penguins didn't tend to have land predators, and they didn't usually hurt themselves falling over on the ice. It must have been something more serious, like a close call with a leopard seal.

The quacking and honking sound of the colony calmed down, and Callie could see that more parents had arrived. Most of them were rounding up their chicks and guiding them back to the nests. Almost all the chicks had two parents, and they huddled together in their stone circles. Something was happening....

Callie felt the wind suddenly pick up again. To her right, she saw a huge black cloud swiftly approaching, and within seconds, it was above them. Snowflakes began to fall. Not like they had in her yard, sprinkle-soft. These flakes came in sideways and fast. In minutes, it was impossible to see anything.

Callie retreated to the research station. Penguins were built for this, but she wasn't. She really wanted some hot chocolate.

Waddling Away

Inside the station, Callie found packets of hot chocolate powder and a kettle. Just what she needed!

With hands around her mug, she sat on a couch and watched the blizzard through one of the round windows. She couldn't see the penguins now, or even the black mountains. Just the blinding-white gusts that swirled and swept across the landscape. And then, as quickly as it had arrived, the snow was gone.

Callie jumped up and pressed her nose against the glass. "Where are you, little Adélie penguins?" she wondered, searching the shore. But it wasn't a waddling mass anymore. There was only white. "Where did you go?"

With a giant quiver, the mass of penguins shook off the snow that clung to their backs, revealing their beautiful dark feathers once again.

Callie breathed a sigh of relief. For a moment she'd thought they had somehow gotten swept away, but of course they hadn't. They were penguins, and this was their land. If they could take care of themselves so well, then why was she here?

It must have something to do with keeping these Adélies safe, she thought. *But what?*

She didn't have time to think about it for long before a movement down on the shore caught her eye. Not a bustling motion like before. This time it looked like the colony was forming a line. Callie watched as they stretched across the landscape, like spilled black paint. The penguins were on the move!

Callie grabbed the binoculars. The parents were bustling around, steering the chicks ahead of them. This wasn't playtime; it was an organized march. Callie was so fascinated that she was frozen to the spot, even when the silence inside the station was interrupted by the crackle of the communication radio. She made herself listen to the voices. There were two scientists talking. Maybe she would find out why she was here.

"Copy that…. The pack ice is completely broken up and coming ashore."

"It's not a surprise. The temperature is way above the norm for this time of year, which means the ice is breaking up. The warm air is bringing rain. A cold front turned it to snow just now—did you see it? Every year it's getting worse. I worry about the penguins."

"They've started their migration north. I've seen three colonies on the move."

"Let's hope they make it past the pack ice."

Callie, who had been watching the blipping lights on the radio transmitter, turned back to the window. *So that's what's happening*, she thought as the final few penguins left the rock nests down by the shore. *They're migrating!*

Callie knew that migration was a natural thing to do. Obviously she wasn't here to help them on their way, so maybe she was here for another reason. She was sad about that—she'd have liked to spend more time with the penguins. But while she tried to figure out why she *was* here, she decided to go and collect some of the soft gray feathers that the chicks had left behind.

She raided the medicine cabinet and found lip balm to keep her lips from cracking. She put on sunscreen, too. Even though it was freezing, the sun was super bright. With a dry hat and gloves, she stepped out of the research station and walked carefully on the slippery new snow back down to the shore. There had been no snow boots her size at the research station, and the treads on her rain boots had worn down. With every step, she arched back or doubled-over forward, trying to get her balance. Then she heard the sound of laughter.

Were the scientists back? Were they making fun of her?

She spun around, but there was no sign of anyone on the balcony. So where was that sound coming from? There it was again. A honk, this time. It was just like the honk that the clumsy little penguin had made....

It *was* the clumsy little penguin!

Standing alone in a stone circle, it stuck out its neck and honked again. And again. The little bird was calling. All the others were gone. Callie felt tears spring to her eyes—it had been left behind! She quickly wiped her tears away and thought about what to do. She could take the penguin inside and take care of it. But she knew that sometimes it wasn't good to interfere. She shouldn't do anything until she understood exactly what had happened.

She walked up close to the penguin and crouched down next it. Callie remembered her school trip to the zoo

35

and how she'd learned that chicks could only be told apart by their calls, and that male chicks grew larger and fatter than females. This one was on the small side, with slightly stumpy flippers and a short beak, so it was probably a girl. It cocked its head to the side and made her smile.

"What are we going to do with you?" she said to the little penguin.

It honked and waddled closer to her. Then it backed away. It walked toward her again and barked in her face before running off. Callie laughed and held out her hand, encouraging it closer.

"It's okay. I won't hurt you," she said. "I'm a friendly human. My name is Callie, and I love animals. What's your name?"

The penguin made a quacking sound.

"How about I call you Una. It means 'one.' And you really are a special one, aren't you!"

Callie reached out her hand farther and rubbed Una's soft tummy. An urgent and angry squawk burst through the cold air. Callie turned to see a larger penguin waddling through the stone nests, shrieking in annoyance. It was running as fast as it could, but an injured leg was slowing it down. It was the mother!

Callie stood back and allowed the parent penguin to greet her lost child. They must have been separated during the snowstorm. The mother started pushing Una along, but Una kept wobbling and stumbling on the stones. Then she fell over. With the mother being so protective, there was nothing Callie could do. She watched helplessly as they tripped and fell, tripped and fell. In the distance, the last hobbling penguins of the migration pack were barely visible on the horizon. They'd never catch up! Callie buried her face in her gloved hands and fought back the tears.

Callie knew she was here to help, but how?

Then she felt something tugging at
her coat. Tug, tug.

Callie looked down. It was the mother.
She tugged, looked up, and put her
head to one side…. She was asking for
help! Una fell on her tummy again and
honked twice. It sounded like "ma-ma."

"Of course I'll help you, Mama!"
Callie said. "Just tell me what to do."

Breaking Ice

Callie followed Mama over to Una, who'd managed to get up on her feet. Mama butted her along with her soft tummy, but it only made Una wobble and topple over. Callie could sense Mama's frustration.

"Maybe it would be quicker if I just carried Una for you," she said, placing her hands around the penguin chick.

Una was about the size of Emma's cat, Patches, whom she picked up a lot. Patches was all wriggling legs and tail, but this felt completely different. Una was like a smooth, solid rock. She flapped her flippers as she was lifted up and Callie laughed, pulling the little penguin close to her chest.

"You're built for swimming, not flying, so don't even try!"

Una honked happily, but Mama wasn't quite so happy. She barked aggressively and began slapping Callie's legs with her hard flippers.

"Okay, okay, I'll put her down," Callie said calmly, placing Una on the ground.

Mama continued to strut around her, and it was hard not to laugh. Even when they were angry, penguins were funny and very sweet. But Callie knew that animals had different rules of behavior, and she had to respect the rules. Resisting the urge to cuddle animals was going to be one of the hardest things about being a vet! If Mama didn't trust her, Callie knew she would have to earn that trust. Besides, it was normal for a parent to be protective.

Finally, Mama calmed down and stood still. She wasn't showing any signs of trying to catch up with the migrating colony. Callie wondered if she had changed her mind and decided to stay at the nesting site. However, it was almost the end of summer—winter was on its way. Without the warmth and protection of all those other penguins, how would they survive? Callie thought about building them a big nest and filling it with the molted feathers, just to give them the best chance…. Then Mama started walking again.

This time, she wasn't heading after the others. She was making her way toward the ocean. Una flipped and flopped behind her. Callie didn't know what to do.

Mama stopped and looked at her. She honked.

"You want me to come with you?"

Mama honked again.

"All right," Callie said, smiling with

relief. "I want to help you—I really do."

They stood on the very edge of the
shore, where great chunks of pack ice had
floated in and stacked up against each
other, like giant quartz crystals. It made it
hard for a penguin as small as an Adélie to
find a quick route into the water. Mama
hopped up onto a piece of ice, then onto
another one next to it. It had stacked itself
at an angle, and it was hard for Mama to
stand up. Una tried to follow but Mama
waddled back, shooing her baby away
with her flippers and barking until Una
was safely on the shore. Mama tried to get
into the water again.

"You're getting food!" Callie realized.
"Great idea, Mama. Una could use
energy. I'll keep her here, I promise."

Mama hopped forward—from one ice

block to the next—looking for a way
into the water. Una tried to follow, so
Callie ran forward and stood, blocking
her way. Una ran around her. It became
a funny game. Una moved. Callie
blocked. They ran up and down the
shoreline, honking and laughing.

"I bet you'd be good at chess,"
Callie said. "You definitely like playing
games, don't you?"

Una tilted her head to one side.
Honk, honk!

"I wonder how your mom is doing,"
Callie said, looking out over the ice.
They had moved down the shoreline a
little, and there was less ice here—just
a block or two—and there was a clear
view of the ocean beyond. Somewhere
beneath the surface, Mama was fishing.
Callie shivered at the thought of that
ice-cold water as she turned back
around.

"Hey, you!"

While Callie had been gazing out
to sea, Una had hopped onto a block
of sea ice and flopped down on her

tummy. The little penguin chick slid one way, then used her flippers to rotate her body so she could slide back again. Callie clapped her hands. Who needs to stand up when you can slide on your belly!

"Great job, Una!" she cried. Una honked back happily.

Suddenly there was a giant *snap!* A *crack!* The noise of grating ice. The ice block was breaking! Una stood up and wobbled as the piece she was standing on broke away and drifted from the shore. Luckily its route out to sea was blocked by ice floes—large sheets of flat ice, but Callie saw how dangerous the situation could become.

There was another penguin fact she remembered from the zoo—chicks aren't entirely waterproof until they have all their grown-up feathers. Una could freeze if she fell into the ice-cold water.

"Una!" Callie shouted. "Don't slide. Don't wobble. I'll come and get you!"

Callie took off her glove and touched the water beneath the ice blocks. It was so cold it stung her skin. She knew she couldn't get wet in these freezing temperatures without doing herself some damage. And she wouldn't be able to help these penguins if she was hurt.

But what else could she do? Una was drifting farther and farther out to sea, and Mama was still nowhere to be seen.

The Threat of Seals

The longer Callie stood not knowing what to do, the less chance there was of saving Una. The ice block had stopped beside another, larger one. It would only take a big wave to split them apart, then Una, stuck on her iceberg island, would move quickly out into the ocean.

Callie had to think quickly. She had to think like a vet faced with an emergency and use whatever was available. She had nothing with her that would help save

Una, although there might be things back at the research station.

Callie turned and started running.

Una honked. It sounded high-pitched and scared.

"I'm coming back, Una, I promise!" Callie called, waving.

She continued to run as fast as she could, tripping on rocks and skidding on patches of frozen snow that now covered the area. Una's distress calls rang in her ears, and Callie wanted more than anything to comfort the penguin, but she couldn't stop. There wasn't a moment to lose.

The research station was so cozy inside, and it would have been wonderful to warm up with some hot chocolate. But there was no time for that. Instead, Callie worked fast, rummaging through the cupboards. She had no idea how she was going to rescue Una, so she just took anything she thought might be useful. She put it all in a pile in the middle of the floor. A few cans of fish, in case Mama had no luck fishing. Binoculars. Cookies for energy. A length of rope. A pickaxe. An aluminium blanket for keeping in body heat. Spare gloves and socks.

There was too much to stuff in the pockets of her snowsuit. She spotted a large backpack hanging on a peg— perfect! She put the smaller items inside and tied the pickaxe and the fishing net to the straps.

Then she ran, slipping and tripping under the weight of the pack, down to the shore. Una hadn't drifted far, but the ice blocks that had been keeping her trapped had moved. Now there was nothing stopping Una from drifting out into the ocean. Una was standing absolutely still, and Callie's heart thumped to see the baby penguin looking so alone. She seemed so tiny against the huge backdrop of the sea and the towering ice that floated by, slow, steady, and unstoppable.

"I'm here, Una!" she called.

Honk, honk!

"That's right, Una. Honk, honk!"
Callie shouted cheerily, hoping it would
make the penguin feel better.

Honk, honk. Honk. Honk, honk, honk.

"I'm here, Una!" Callie called again.
"And I'm going to find a way to get

you back!"

But Una's honking didn't stop, and Callie could now see a dark shape in the water next to her. Maybe it was Mama, returned from fishing. Una was probably excited.

Honk, honk.

The little penguin's call didn't sound like one of happiness. It was one of alarm. Callie grabbed the binoculars to get a better look. She twisted the dials to get them in focus and ... now she could see clearly that it wasn't Mama in the water. It was a leopard seal. A small one—but even small leopard seals were predators. And this one's sights were set on baby Una.

"Get away from her!" Callie shouted. "Leave her alone. Hey, seal!"

The leopard seal ignored Callie's screams as it continued to circle the ice. Una was running from one side of the block to the other in fear. If she fell and slipped off into the sea…. Callie couldn't bear to think about it.

The seal started to heave itself up onto the ice. Callie looked at the predator again through the binoculars.

The leopard seal was dappled gray and white, its skin as smooth as a pebble. Every time it flung itself onto the ice, it bounced back like a giant water balloon. This was an inexperienced pup and probably hadn't done much hunting—but poor Una didn't know that. She was terrified, and her panicky squeals intensified every time the seal came close.

Come on, Callie, think of something!
Callie took deep breaths and thought
about the situation. Vets always
had to take animals' feelings into
consideration—and there were two
animals in this situation.

The leopard seal wasn't going to give
up. Why? Because it was hungry. This
animal needed to eat, just like any other.

Of course! Callie threw the backpack
on the ground and looked inside for the

canned fish. It was supposed to be for Una to eat. But it was needed right now.

Callie peeled the lid off one can and threw the contents into the ocean as hard as she could. The chunks of fish fell into the water with a *plop!* right next to the seal. It let go of Una's ice to investigate and guided the sinking fish back to the surface of the water with its flipper. It began to eat. Excellent! Callie quickly grabbed another can. This time, she deliberately didn't aim it at the seal. The fish bobbed a short distance from the ice block before starting to sink. The seal had seen it, though, and followed. Callie emptied the final can and threw it way off in another direction to lure the leopard seal away. The seal slunk under the water and disappeared.

Now she had to get Una back. Who knew how many hungry leopard seals were out there, waiting for a penguin snack? Even though the little penguin wasn't far away, Callie couldn't go in the water. Somehow she would have to bring the ice back to shore. Callie looked at the items on the ground where she had thrown the backpack and noticed the rope and the pickaxe. She had an idea.

Callie put the backpack back on to give her more weight. Then with one end of the rope tied around her tummy and the other around the pickaxe, she lifted and held the pickaxe over her head, waiting for the perfect moment.... When Una had moved far enough to one side of the iceberg, out of harm's way, Callie threw the pickaxe with all her might. It flew through the air, taking a length of rope with it, and struck the ice perfectly.

"That's it, Una! We did it!" Callie cried happily, pulling the rope carefully so that Una didn't fall off the ice block.

She pulled the ice back to the shore and beckoned Una to hop onto land. But the poor penguin was terrified by her experience and refused to move.

"Come on, little one," Callie said. "You're safe now." She leaned forward over the ice to pet Una and show her that everything was okay, but Una shuffled backward. Callie leaned farther. She would have to grab Una, hold her tightly, and hope that Mama didn't get angry.

"Una, I'm your friend—whoops!"

Callie's foot slipped on the icy wash at her feet. She fell onto the ice block. It rocked under her weight, tipping forward on the swell of the wave, and then it moved. Out into the water. Out to sea.

Oh, no, Callie thought. *This isn't good at all.*

Slip-Sliding Playtime

When it had just held Una, the ice had looked stable. But now, with Callie's weight as well, it rocked like an ice cube in soda. Callie lay absolutely still, but Una was still jumpy from her brush with the leopard seal. She was padding up and down, tilting them backward and forward. Callie knew that any big movement would tip them both into the freezing water.

"Hey, Una, it's going to be okay," she

said soothingly, although she wasn't sure she believed it. They were floating out to sea—how was everything going to be okay?

"You'll see," she continued. "It won't be long until ... until...."

A-ha! Callie carefully rose to her feet, balancing on the block of ice as though it was a surfboard.

"Until we find a bigger home!" she finished, wrenching the tip of the pickaxe free.

Up ahead was a larger block of ice. It would be like a raft, big enough for both of them. And although they weren't exactly home safe and dry, it would take away the immediate worry so Callie could think about what to do next.

Using her new pick-and-pull method,
Callie threw the pickaxe at the bigger
iceberg and dragged their little raft
closer to it. Una seemed to understand
and sprang to life. Waddling at full
speed, she leaped onto the new, bigger
iceberg, landing with a *thwack* on her
tummy. She started skidding playfully.
It was like her very own ice rink!

Callie stepped across more carefully, fearful of slipping at the last moment as she had done before. Only this time she'd be falling into deep, freezing water.

The ice was thick and sturdy and hardly rocked when Callie put her weight on it. She stood at the edge, watching her little friend slide around. It reminded her that right now, she should be back home, sliding down the street on plastic bags with Emma. Her brief sadness was brushed away when Una honked a happy *honk*. The penguin was waddling toward her.

"You want me to come and play? Okay, Una!"

Callie stepped forward, but the ice was slippery, and she couldn't find a way to stand up straight without wobbling.

"Uh-oh!" she said, feeling her balance go. She jerked forward, then backward, and then forward again, falling onto the ice with a big smack. Thank goodness for her puffy snowsuit—without it, she'd be covered in bruises! Una honked and Callie laughed, unable to stand as her feet slid around like a beginner ice-skater.

Una stood next to her and flapped her flippers. Her honk was more of a cackle now. For a tired little penguin, Una certainly managed to find enough energy to have fun!

"I know I look ridiculous," Callie said, finally managing to stand upright. Una waddled from side to side on the spot. "You look ridiculous, too!"

Then Callie fell again—*thwack!*—and Una cackled so hard that it became infectious. Soon Callie was giggling helplessly, which made getting up again impossible. Una circled her, peering at her with curiosity and nuzzling her neck.

When her fit of giggles was over, Callie stood up. Once again, Una waddled on the spot in front of her. Oh … this was a lesson: Una was teaching her how to walk on ice! Callie watched carefully and copied Una. She leaned forward so her body weight was right above the front foot. Next, she leaned sideways and brought the back foot alongside the front, moving her body weight across. She did it again. It was slow, but it worked. She was waddling!

"I'm doing it, Una!" Callie said
gleefully. "I'm walking like a penguin!"

Una showed her pleasure by falling onto
her stomach and skidding across the ice.

"I'm not doing that!" Callie laughed,
wobbling slightly as she lost her
concentration. "I'd look more like a
walrus!"

Callie marveled at how funny Una could look one minute with her waddling walk, and how graceful she could look the next, gliding as smooth and fast as a bobsled. Up and down the ice she went, while Callie clapped and cheered! And then Una didn't turn in time, maybe because she was weaker than usual. She slid right off the edge of the ice and into the ocean.

Callie knew she didn't have time to waddle to the edge—after all, she was still a beginner—so she threw herself onto her stomach and skidded to the place where Una had fallen in. Looking over the edge into the dark blue water, she couldn't see anything. Then Una's little black-and-white figure appeared beneath the surface. Callie waved, signaling to Una that she was there, and Una shot out of the water. The leap wasn't powerful enough to get up onto the ice, though, and she fell back in.

"Try again! You can do it!" Callie called.

The penguin flapped her flippers and propelled herself toward the ice again. But she was tired—all the playing around had worn her out. As Una fell back in, Callie spotted something else a few feet away. A flash of black-and-white in the water. It was much too big to be Mama. And it was getting bigger and bigger.

Oh, no!

"Una! You have to hurry!" Callie shrieked. "Una! Jump now!"

Callie looked down at the struggling

penguin and then up again at the approaching shape. The dorsal fin cut through the surface, and the huge curve of its back breached the water, black and shiny. It was an orca—otherwise known as a killer whale. And it was coming toward them.

Danger in the Water

Una was weak, and there was no time to hesitate. Two, three seconds at most is all it would take for the orca to reach the ice. And Callie knew what would happen to Una if it did.

She yanked off her gloves and plunged her hands into the water. Pain seared through her skin, as if it was burning, but she couldn't give up. If she didn't save Una, she would never be able to forgive herself.

Clenching
her teeth
through
the pain
and
pushing away
the fear as she felt
her hands turning numb, she grabbed
the baby penguin. With a yell of might,
Callie pulled her up and out of the
water. Holding Una against her chest,
she quickly shuffled backward on her
bottom toward the center of the ice raft,
just as the orca's rubbery fin slid by.
That was close!

"Are you a-a-a-l-l r-r-right?" Callie's
teeth chattered. There was no happy
honk or cackle. The penguin was frozen
with fear. "I-I-I'm g-g-oing to put you

d-d-down," she stammered.

Callie placed Una next to her and fumbled with the backpack. The icy water had made her hands stop working, so using her teeth, Callie pulled on her fleece-lined gloves. As her hands warmed up and the numbness wore off, pain ran through her fingers. Although it hurt, she knew this was a good sign. It meant her hands weren't damaged and would soon be working normally again.

Boom. There was loud bang, and the ice rocked violently. Callie looked up to see the orca's fin still alongside the edge of the iceberg. It had rammed into it! A cold chill ran up her spine when she realized what the whale was doing.

Callie had seen wildlife documentaries about killer whales. They were intelligent, and they had hunting strategies. They also hunted in groups. She spun around to see if there were others, but the ocean was calm and blue. It looked as if this one was on its own. It wouldn't be able to climb onto the ice, like the leopard seal, but it had something else in mind. It was going to tip the ice over.

The orca rolled onto its side, revealing how big it was. Its enormous fin pointed skyward, like a towering mountain. It rolled back again, smacking the water and creating a mighty wave that rocked the iceberg backward. The pack ice had felt so strong before, but now it was being tossed around like a sailboat on a rough sea. The orca rolled onto its side once more.

"Una, stand up! Don't lie down," Callie said, knowing that if they lost their balance, they would slip off the ice and into the water. "I need to make a safe place for us."

Una had been screeching and flapping when the seal was around, but now she was very tired and frightened. She certainly wasn't in the mood to play slip-slide on her tummy. She stood on her flat feet and shuffled nervously as Callie set to work with the pickaxe. She dug at a point in the center of the ice. If she could make a hole for them to sit in, they wouldn't be thrown off as easily, and maybe the orca would lose interest. Callie wasn't sure if it would work, but it was the only chance they had. She chipped away at the ice.

The orca made another enormous wave. Callie yelled, and with one hand, she held onto the axe, which she had just dug into the ice, and with the other she grabbed Una's flipper. Phew! But they might not be so lucky next time.

"Quick, Una!" Callie said, pulling the penguin into the hole she had dug. "Sit in here."

The orca slammed the ice again, but though Callie had managed to get Una safely into the hole, she slipped. Her legs slid out from underneath her, but she just managed to grip the edge of the hole as her body slid down the ice.

The ice settled, and when Callie looked up, the orca was gone. Her heart was beating like a drum, her mouth was dry, and her lungs were burning from breathing fast in the cold, cold air. She shakily slid herself to the edge of the ice and looked out over the water. The huge dark shape of the orca was finally moving away.

Callie sat up and watched it go, breathing a sigh of relief. Una waddled up to her and stood close. She seemed to understand that Callie needed to see a friendly face.

Honk!

"Oh, Una," Callie said. "That was close, wasn't it?"

Honk! Honk!

Callie rubbed the little penguin's head, noticing that the few chick feathers that still clung to it were soaking wet. Some were even forming ice crystals. Callie grabbed a towel from her backpack and

rubbed Una's
head until all the
water was gone.

"Come here,
fuzzy head," she
said affectionately,
pulling Una toward
her. She wrapped her arms around
her little friend. "Who would have
thought you and I would have such an
adventure!"

They sat together quietly, looking out
to sea, catching their breath.

Now that the drama was over, Callie
couldn't help thinking how lucky she
had been. Not just to survive, but to
actually see a killer whale in the wild!
Callie had never thought she'd get
to see one. And now she had—the

smooth marble of its white tummy and its jet-black back, and even its beady eyes. It was incredible. Although she thought that one close encounter with a killer whale was probably enough for a lifetime!

But then she saw a ripple on the surface beyond the ice. There was something else in the water. A smaller creature this time—dark, with a flash of white.

Learning to Fish

It was Mama! When she saw Una, she came zooming toward the ice as fast as she could. She shot out of the water and landed next to Callie.

"Great job, Mama!" said Callie, crying with relief. She held out her arms to take the poor, terrified penguin in a hug. But Mama was up on her feet, slapping Callie away. She wanted to see her child. Callie was heartened to see that Mama's injuries didn't get in the way of her survival instinct. Or her determination.

Mama rushed up to Una and brushed her neck against the little penguin, but she didn't open her beak wide or lower her head. It was clear she hadn't found any food, though it was not surprising as the ocean was full of predators. It was a miracle that she'd actually made it back alive. Now Una needed something to give her energy, quickly. Callie wished she hadn't used all the canned fish to lure away the leopard seal.

Suddenly, Mama looked alert and waddled to the edge of the ice. She had spotted something. Callie hoped it wasn't another killer whale—she didn't know if she had the energy to save them all again. But Mama didn't honk with alarm. Instead, she turned to Callie and flapped her flippers. Then she turned back to face the water.

"What can you see, Mama?" Callie said, penguin-waddling as carefully as she could to the edge.

Ahead of them, a smoky pink cloud bloomed in the dark blue waters of the ocean. As the pink patch floated closer, Callie saw that it was made up of very small creatures. Teeny tiny shrimp. Millions of them. Krill!

"It's food, Mama!" Callie cried happily. However, getting back in the water wasn't something Mama wanted to do, not with sharp-toothed predators lurking below the surface. Callie looked at her pile of equipment. Her fishing net was still tied to the backpack. "I have an idea," she said.

The holes in her fishing net were too large, though, and the krill slipped through, and Mama soon lost interest in Callie's attempts at fishing. She waddled back to where Una was sitting in the hole. She nudged Una out and started pecking at the ice, making the hole deeper. Callie didn't know what she was doing, but she did know that Mama had strong survival instincts. She watched as the big penguin pecked hard at the ice. If she kept on going, she'd break through!

Callie gasped. "That's what you're trying to do! You're making a fishing hole! Let me help."

Mama was bossy and kept flipper-slapping Callie as she tried to get to the hole. Eventually Callie nudged her aside and was able to quickly finish the job with her pickaxe. They stood together in the middle of the floating ice, looking through the hole at the water beneath. Occasionally waves lapped up through it. The bloom of krill was getting closer, and it wouldn't be much longer until it was right beneath the iceberg.

Mama and Una would have all the food they needed to restore their energy without the danger of a deep-sea dive.

Although their troubles weren't over yet, Callie allowed herself a moment of rest. She sat down, ate a couple of cookies, and swapped her ice-encrusted gloves with the spare ones she had packed. Then she watched, tired and happy, as her friendly penguins filled themselves on krill. Mama would stick her head into the hole, gobble up a load of shrimp, and drop it into Una's wide-open mouth. It certainly wasn't the most pleasant thing to watch, but Callie knew it was all part of nature: a mother feeding her young.

Within minutes, both Una and
Mama were looking brighter. When
they had finished eating, Mama did a
mighty shake, spraying water droplets
everywhere. After that, she looked as
dry as if she'd never plunged into the
ocean. Una, however, was shivering.
With the water dripping from Mama,
and the sea spray that showered them
every time the water lapped at the ice,
Una was finding it hard to stay dry.
She was starting to freeze.

History Lessons

Callie wrapped the aluminium blanket around Una, but it wasn't soft and floppy like a normal blanket, and it wouldn't stay on the chick's shoulders without Callie holding it there. That wasn't something Mama was happy about—she cuddled up close to her baby, smothering her with her chest feathers. It wasn't enough—Una was still shaking with cold. Mama looked up at Callie and shuffled around a little.

She was making room for her!

Feeling honored, Callie huddled with the penguins, glad to be able to give them a little more warmth. But if the temperature dropped any farther or if they ended up in the water again, they'd be in trouble. Callie needed to get them back on land and find help.

"Hold on tight. I'm just going to look for ice floes."

The shore on which the New Captain Scott Research Station stood was now far behind them—they had drifted quite a way on their iceberg. Rather than fighting the flow of the ocean, Callie knew that their best chance of survival was to get onto the nearest shore and walk. There was a headland up ahead of them, and plenty of floating ice to use as stepping stones to get there.

Callie stepped forward and slipped, sprawling on the ice like a sea star. She briefly imagined Kamal laughing at her and suddenly felt very far from home. She pushed the thought away. She could worry about that when she got these penguins to safety. That's clearly what she was here to do.

In the meantime, if she was going to be moving across the ice quickly, throwing and pulling the pickaxe, the skidding was definitely going to be a problem. So she started chipping little holes across the iceberg to break up the surface and give her places where she could dig in the toes of her boots. Una and Mama huddled together and watched. Now that Callie had helped with the fishing hole, it seemed Mama trusted her a little more.

With her pickaxe, Callie pulled the first chunk of ice toward them. "Come on," she said, heaving the backpack over her shoulder. "Follow me."

She stepped carefully onto the next block and waited for the penguins to follow. Despite being so cold, Una flopped down on her tummy and skidded playfully across onto the new ice floe.

"Be careful!" Callie laughed. "You don't want to fall into the water again. Your turn, Mama!"

Callie and Una stood on the iceberg and waited for Mama. But Mama hadn't seen Callie's pick-and-pull method of getting across the ice before and hesitated, honking angrily at them as if they were naughty children. When she realized that Una wasn't coming back, she reluctantly waddled across.

"You're going to have to be quicker than that," Callie said, shaking her head. "We've got a long way to go."

Carefully, steadily, Callie created icy stepping stones, and they made their way across the bay to the headland. The ice wasn't as stacked up here, and they managed to reach the shore without difficulty, although Una was very weak. It was only her playful nature that kept her going. She was shuddering with the cold, and her movements were becoming jerky. Callie was about to pick her up, despite Mama's protectiveness, when she saw a solid shape in the distance.

"There's a building over there!" Callie cried. "Maybe it's another research station. They'll be able to help! Come on, Una. Come on, Mama. Keep going!"

But the building wasn't a research station. Callie wanted to cry as she saw its old wooden walls—it was just a hut! Dragging her feet, she walked up to it and wiped the ice from a plaque on the wall. *Shackleton's Hut.*

"Another explorer." She sighed. "It's an amazing part of history, but that doesn't help us much, does it? Come on. Let's go inside and see if there's anything that isn't rotten."

Callie pushed the door open. The hut was surprisingly cozy. The sunlight that streamed through the window had warmed the air inside. There were blankets and mattresses. There were cans of food on the shelves. It was old, but it was perfectly intact. Callie laughed with relief and quietly thanked Ernest Shackleton and his adventurers for building such a sturdy hut. Now she had to get the penguins comfortable and dry, which was hard when Mama was still so protective. Poor Mama. She probably never dreamed she'd be teaming up with a human that looked like a puffy yeti!

Callie took off her giant snowsuit and saw the penguins' curious faces as she halved in size.

"Yep, this is me," Callie laughed. "Much smaller in real life!"

Concerned about the freezing temperatures, Callie's first job was to make sure that they all recovered from their adventures out on the water. Mama had given herself a big shake, but Una was looking a bit bedraggled. Callie found an old blanket and rubbed the little penguin down until she was totally dry. They were all safe. For now.

Callie was suddenly overcome with tiredness. Her arms were exhausted from lifting the pickaxe, her entire body ached from the cold that had crept through the puffy layers of her snowsuit, and her mind was strained from being alert for hours.

What time is it? she wondered. It was still bright outside, but her eyes felt heavy, as if it were evening time.

She remembered that at the North and South Poles, it was impossible to time your days by sunrise and sunset. In summer, they had six months of sun, and in winter, six months of darkness. Now Callie didn't know whether to let herself fall asleep or stay awake!

She smiled at Una and Mama, who were snuggling against each other tightly, and thought of her own parents. She missed them. She missed home.... How would she get back there? Why was she still here? If it was to rescue these sweet Adélie penguins, her job was done, wasn't it? There must be something else she had to do.

To stop herself from falling asleep, Callie got up and looked for some food.

There were still some cookies left over in her backpack. She ate them as she paced around the hut, searching for clues.

There was a book on the table. It was open to a page with spiky handwriting. The ink had faded and it was hard to read, but Callie saw that it was dated 1917 —more than a hundred years ago! It was a diary entry by one of the men on Shackleton's expedition, maybe even Shackleton himself. It talked of the stress and loneliness of being at the South Pole. Callie recognized some of the descriptions and feelings, and she decided that if even these strong explorers found it difficult, then she had been very brave indeed. And she was definitely capable of being a vet in all situations!

There was another section to the diary entry. It described the Adélie penguin migration. The writer said he had watched it pass by this very hut— thousands and thousands of penguins!

"Wow!" Callie said aloud. "For centuries, the migrations have been taking place right here, following in the footsteps of the generations of penguins before them...."

Callie looked across at her two beautiful penguins, who were looking back at her, blinking in the stream of sunlight through the window.

"Migration is in your blood. It's part of your life. *This* is my task, isn't it?" It was more of a realization than a question, and Callie nodded at her friends. "I need to reunite you with your colony. You have to join the migration!"

But how?

Joining the Migration

Callie looked through the journal for more details. All she could find out was that the Adélies went north at the end of the summer to a warmer climate and better feeding grounds. There had to be something else in Shackleton's hut that could help her. But the hut was old, and she could only see books and scrolls of paper.

Callie unrolled a scroll. The paper was yellowed and crinkly, and she had to secure it to the table with a kettle and a cup to keep it from curling up again. It was a map of Ross Island. Shackleton had marked the position of his hut with a box and his name scrawled above it.

If the Adélie colony that the writer had seen had started their migration outside Captain Scott's old hut, there was a good chance that Una and Mama's colony would be taking the same route. If they were, they'd be passing Shackleton's hut. Maybe they had done so already. If they had, there would be footprints in the earth and in the snow....

Callie ran outside. No footprints. Was it possible that they had crossed the bay on their ice floes faster than the penguins could walk? Maybe, just maybe, they were in the right place at the right time!

Then, carried on the thin air, came a cacophony of honking, like a distant traffic jam. Callie stared until dots danced in front of her eyes. She blinked. They weren't dots. They were penguins!

"It's the front of the migration line!" she gasped.

Callie ran back into the hut, a huge grin on her face. "Quick, Mama, your colony is coming. Quick, quick!"

The penguins sensed Callie's excitement and started waddling around the hut crazily like bouncy balls. Callie took the opportunity to give Una a last rub down with the towel—she needed to be in the best condition to tackle the migration ahead of her. As the towel dropped to the floor, so did the last of

Una's baby feathers. In front of Callie stood a sleek, black-and-white, fully waterproof chick.

"You're perfect," Callie said, a tear springing to her eye. "Hey!"

Mama was bustling around Callie's legs, but this time her flippers weren't beating her back. Instead, they were pushing Una forward between her legs. Callie sniffed back her tears and laughed as Una snuggled in, and Mama, now completely trusting, wrapped her flippers around Callie's shins. They stood like that for a minute, and Callie savored every moment of the group hug. She knew this was good-bye. Once Una and Mama had joined the colony, her time with the playful Adélie chick and her incredible, brave mother would be over.

"We've been through so much together! It's hard to leave you," Callie said. "But you need to be with your colony. And I need to be with mine."

Mama gave a gentle honk and stepped back, leaving Callie and Una to share one last cuddle together.

"You, too, now, Una," Callie said, gulping back tears. "You're going to be just fine."

Through the window, the first bobbing heads of the migrating penguins came into view, and the sound of squabbles and squawks grew louder. Una rocked from side to side. Maybe she could hear her friends. Callie smiled as she remembered seeing them all that first time, stealing stones and chasing each other. It seemed like so long ago when it had actually all been the same day ... or at least, she thought it had!

Callie opened the door. Laughter replaced the tears as hundreds of Adélies trudged past, chattering loudly. She had a deep respect for penguins now that she'd spent some time with them, but they were still so funny!

"Go now," Callie said. "Shoo!"

Mama slapped her leg with a flipper,
but it wasn't a scolding. It was a last show
of contact before she continued north.
Una scuttled after her. Outside, the
funny chick turned and looked at Callie
once more before joining the crowd.

Callie kept her eyes on Una for as long
as possible—on the little penguin who

had survived against all the odds, who loved to slide on her tummy, and whose mother would protect her until she was grown up.

Eventually Callie lost sight of her among the thousands of penguins. But she stood at the door of the hut and stared into the distance long after they'd disappeared over the rocky hill.

"Bye-bye!" she called. "Hope you live happily ever after. Or Adélie ever after!" That sounded like something Emma would say!

Callie wondered if Emma had finished her breakfast and was waiting for her back home…. Without the penguins, the South Pole was a very lonely place.

The wind picked up and began to whip snow and ice crystals through the air. Callie's face stung, and without her snowsuit, she started to feel very cold. She stepped back into Shackleton's hut and shut the door. Out of respect for the great explorer who had provided her with shelter, she decided to clean up the hut. Then she would walk back to the New Captain Scott Research Station. If the old map was right, all she had to do was follow the shore southward. If she couldn't get home any other way, she'd just have to radio for help or sit and wait for one of the scientists to come back.

There was a bang on the door. The wind, maybe? Then came another bang. Followed by another.

Someone was out there. And whoever it was, he or she wasn't giving up.

Adélies in the Yard

Callie's heart thumped. Should she
answer the door and ask for help?
Maybe she'd be in trouble for entering a
historical site without permission! Should
she hide? But if she hid, they might go
away, and this could be her only chance
to get help and find a way home....

Callie walked to the door and placed her
hand on the handle. She looked once more
around the hut that had provided shelter
and warmth and saved the lost Adélie

penguins. Then she opened the door.

There was a *whoosh* of cold air, and Callie had to shut her eyes against the blast of snow. The storm must have closed in very quickly. When she wiped the snow from her eyes, a familiar face was staring at her.

"Gotcha!"

In front of her, Emma was doing a victory dance.

"Emma!" Callie exclaimed, stepping out into the cold.

"Don't complain. It was only a little snowball to say hi. Come on! You and I need to get to work. Kamal and Halima have declared a snow war. We need to be prepared. Do you have a wheelbarrow in there or anything we can use to collect snow?"

Confused, Callie looked behind her, back into Shackleton's hut. Only it wasn't an expedition hut anymore. It was a dusty old shed full of plant pots and tools. She was home. Callie tipped back her head and laughed and laughed.

"What's so funny?" Emma said.

"Incoming!" Kamal's voice shouted.

Emma jumped to the side, and Callie was peppered with the neighbors' snowball ambush, including one right on the nose.

"I'm sorry, Callie!" Kamal said sincerely.

"I'm sorry!" Halima echoed. "I'll tell my brother not to do that again."

But Callie was still laughing. "That's okay, Halima. A little snow never hurt anyone. Besides, it's good experience. Who knows when I might find myself helping an animal stranded in the Antarctic!"

"You'll never move that far away," Emma said huffily.

"Why not? Don't you think I'm strong enough?" Callie challenged, crossing her arms.

"Of course you are. I just wouldn't let you go. I'd miss you too much, that's all."

"I missed you, too, Emma," Callie smiled, ignoring her friend's confused face. "Now, let's come up with a plan to get Kamal back!"

Emma and Callie spent all morning and afternoon having snowball fights and sledding races down the street, only stopping when Emma wanted to go inside and warm up. Callie felt fine. It was cold, but it wasn't *that* cold!

When the sun began to set at four o'clock, it took Callie by surprise. She had been in daylight for so long, she had forgotten how the snow glowed an eerie blue when the light faded, and how the temperature dropped when the sun disappeared.

"I hope it snows again tonight," said Emma.

"Me, too," Callie agreed. "But we should build something to celebrate today, just in case it doesn't."

"A snowman? Great idea!" Emma said, starting to gather snow together in a heap. Callie watched her for a while.

"Why don't we do something a little different?" she suggested. "Like a snow penguin."

"Yeah, a penguin. A big Emperor penguin!"

"Or how about an Adélie penguin instead?" Callie said. "They're small and super cute."

In the dying light, Callie and Emma built up their heap of snow and smoothed it down, carving out feet and flippers and shaping a head. They created a beak with strips of bark. Emma waddled around it, chanting "Snow, snow, penguino" and Callie laughed and rubbed the frozen statue until it was as smooth as a real penguin.

She stood back and looked at it, beaming with pride and feeling emotional as it brought back memories of Una and Mama and their great adventure on the ice floes of the Antarctic. Callie would never be a famous name alongside Scott and Shackleton, but in a way, she had made her mark on the South Pole—she had made sure that two Adélie penguins lived to continue their story.

"Hey, what's that?"

Halima was peering over the fence. Kamal popped up next to her.

"It's an Indian penguin," Emma said proudly.

"An Indian penguin?" Halima laughed. "There's no such thing."

"Well, that's what Callie says, and Callie knows everything about animals."

"I never said it was an Indian penguin, Emma!" Callie said. "Penguins only live in the southern hemisphere. India is in the northern hemisphere."

"But you said it was a Delhi penguin, and everyone knows Delhi is in India."

When Callie realized Emma's mistake, she burst out laughing, and soon the others were laughing, too, although they didn't know why.

"Adélie. It's an *Adélie* penguin, not *a Delhi* penguin!" Callie gasped when she could speak again.

"Adélie!" Emma slapped her hand to her forehead. "I'm such a banana!"

After hot dogs for dinner, Emma's mom came to pick Emma up. She and Callie hugged and crossed their fingers that there'd be two snow days in a row.

When Emma had left, Callie ran upstairs and changed into her pajamas and fluffy slippers. It felt so good to be comfortable and warm again. She snuggled up on the couch with a mug of hot chocolate and watched a documentary about beehives. But she couldn't stop thinking about Una. She got up and pressed her nose against the window.

The yard glistened in the
moonlight—all white, blue, and black.
Her eyes were drawn to the Adélie
penguin. Thanks to the freezing air,
it was still perfect. But next to it
was another mound of snow. Callie
frowned. Hmmm…. What could it be?

Callie opened the back door and
stepped out into the night.

It wasn't a mound of snow…. It was
another penguin! Smaller, but just as
perfect. Oh, wow!
It was Mama and
Una! Callie
stared and
stared, hardly
believing
what she
was seeing.

She stayed there until the mug of hot chocolate in her hands had gotten cold and the snow had begun melting through the soles of her fluffy slippers.

"It was wonderful to see you again. But I've got to go."

She turned to go back inside. Before she closed the door, she looked once again at her Adélie friends and smiled.

"Time to migrate. Don't be late," she whispered.

Snow Una's eyes twinkled back at her like diamonds.

Maybe it was just the moonlight dancing on the snow crystals. Or maybe it was a playful penguin chick saying a last good-bye.

ABOUT THE AUTHOR

Rachel Delahaye was born in Australia but has lived in the UK since she was six years old. She studied linguistics and worked as a magazine writer and editor before becoming a children's author. She loves words and animals; when she can combine the two, she is very happy indeed! At home, Rachel loves to read, write, and watch wildlife documentaries. She loves to go walking in the woods. She also follows news about animal rights and the environment and hopes that one day the world will be a better home for all species, not just humans!

Rachel lives in the beautiful city of Bath, England, with her two lively children and a dog named Rocket.